T0208120

DOTSON

THE DACHSHUND GOES TO THE PARK
EL PERRO SALCHICHA VA AL PARQUE

By/POR
Irene Walshe

ILLUSTRATIONS/ILUSTRACIONES
Laura Liberatore

Archway Publishing books may be ordered through booksellers or by contacting:

Archway Publishing
1663 Liberty Drive
Bloomington, IN 47403
www.archwaypublishing.com
844-669-3957

ISBN: 978-1-6657-1865-3 (sc)
ISBN: 978-1-6657-1864-6 (e)

Print information available on the last page.

Archway Publishing rev. date: 06/17/2022

To my beautiful daughters,
Elena and Elisa.

Dotson the Dachshund goes to the park,
and sees a big balloon with the number ONE.

Dotson el perro salchicha va al parque
y ve un gran globo con el número UNO.

Dotson runs to the ice-cream cart and eats THREE delicious ice-cream cones.

Dotson corre hacia el carro de helados y se come **TRES** deliciosas barquillas.

Dotson stops for a while and sees FOUR funny looking Poodles approaching, but they bark too much and Dotson gets scared.

Dotson se detiene un rato y ve acercarse a **CUATRO** Poodles de aspecto raro, pero ladran mucho y Dotson se asusta.

FIVE squirrels laugh and play as **Dotson** runs fast through the park.

CINCO ardillas ríen y juegan mientras Dotson corre por el parque.

Dotson is lost! He does not recognize the SIX big trees that surround the path.

¡Dotson está perdido! Él no reconoce los
SEIS grandes árboles que rodean el camino.

SEVEN bluebirds tell Dotson where to go.

SIETE azulejos le dicen a Dotson a donde ir.

Dotson sees a man selling EIGHT brightly colored balls and wants to play.

Dotson ve a un señor vendiendo OCHO pelotas de brillantes colores y quiere jugar.

Dotson moves close to the pond and asks **NINE** fish how to get back home.

Dotson se acerca al estanque y les pregunta a **NUEVE** peces cómo regresar a su casa.

TEN marching ants show Dotson the way out of the park.

DIEZ hormigas que marchan le enseñan a Dotson el camino de salida del parque.

Now Dotson sleeps in his fluffy bed, dreaming of the TEN new things he learned today in the park.

Ahora Dotson duerme en su cama mullida y sueña con las **DIEZ** cosas nuevas que aprendió hoy en el parque.

Printed in the United States
by Baker & Taylor Publisher Services